Disney's
THE NEW ADVENTURES OF
WINNIE the POOH
Rabbit Marks the Spot

TWIN BOOKS

MALLARD
PRESS

One day, Winnie the Pooh, Piglet, Tigger and Gopher dressed up like pirates to dig for treasure in Rabbit's garden. When Rabbit saw them digging up his precious vegetables, he was ready to blow his top.

"What is going on here?" demanded Rabbit.

"It's us, Rabbit!" said Pooh, thinking Rabbit didn't recognize them. After all, they were all dressed like pirates.

"We're digging for treasure," explained Gopher.

"Not in *my* garden!" yelled Rabbit.

"Oh, d-dear!" said Piglet, panicking.

KERITS

CABEGE

PUNKINS

BEETS   PEES

Piglet and his gang of pirates ran to their land-ship and shoved off.

"Poop the sail deck!" yelled Captain Piglet. "Swab the mizzenmast! Foot the yardarm!"

Unfortunately, a strong wind blew the land-ship back into the garden. It plowed up all the vegetables, and flattened Rabbit, too.

"I'm not going to get mad," said Rabbit with clenched teeth. "I'm going to teach them a lesson!"

Later that day, in a remote spot somewhere in the Hundred-Acre Wood, Rabbit put the finishing touches on his plan.

"So, Captain Piglet and his pitiful pirates want to find buried treasure, do they?" said Rabbit, shoving a rock-filled chest into a hole. "I'll give them a treasure...a worthless one!"

Rabbit filled the hole with dirt, then grabbed a piece of paper and scrawled something on it.

"I'll even give them a map to help them find it!" he said, grinning. Then he stuffed the map into a bottle, took the bottle to the river, and threw it in.

Not much later, the runaway land-ship crashed on the bank of the river. Pooh looked up and saw a bottle floating toward them. When he waded out to get the bottle, he found that it had Rabbit's map inside. He showed the others.

"Bunny Boy, look what we found!" said Tigger when Rabbit walked up.

"A real treasure map!" said Gopher.

"Why, so you have!" said Rabbit, acting surprised. "This map belonged to my great-great-great uncle Long John Cottontail, a famous pirate!"

"Don't worry, Rabbit," said Tigger. "Findin' treasure's what Captain Piglet and his Pirates do best! Hoo-hoo-hoo!"

Piglet studied the map, then set out to find the treasure. Pooh and the others joined the search, while Rabbit watched from a distance, laughing.

"Now, let's see," said Piglet. "Twelve paces from the river…then turn right, twenty-two steps to the old hollow log…ten paces from the rock, then—"

"Wait a minute!" said Tigger, cutting Piglet off. "Long John Cottontail didn't mean those little piglety paces. He meant big piratey steps!" Tigger took the map from Piglet. "Let's see, six paces to the tree…"

Tigger's paces led straight into Rabbit's front room. He and the others pulled out their shovels and started digging.

"Hiya, Rabbit!" called Tigger when Rabbit appeared at the front door.

Rabbit sputtered, waving his arms wildly as he looked at the huge hole in the middle of his room. He was so furious, he couldn't speak.

"Don't worry, Fluffy-Face," said Tigger, thinking Rabbit was worried about being left out. "When we find the treasure, we'll split it with ya!"

"Aaaarrrrrgh!" screamed Rabbit.

Rabbit grabbed the map and led the group back into the wood.

"Don't you pirates know how to read a map?" asked Rabbit. He came to a stop and pointed to a large X painted in the dirt. "*There's* the X that marks the spot!" said Rabbit.

Tigger, excited, hugged everyone. "The treasure! We found it, and it's exakakly what I always dreamed of! My very own big 'X'!"

Rabbit sighed impatiently. "The treasure's *under* the 'X', Tigger."

"Oh," said Tigger.

Pooh, Piglet, Gopher and Tigger dug until they hit something solid.

"We found it!" cried Piglet, brushing the dirt off the treasure chest.

"Well, what are we waiting for?" asked Gopher. "Let's get it open!"

"W-wait!" said Piglet. "Maybe we should take it to a safe place first."

Tigger agreed. "We better stash it somewhere else," he suggested.

"Somewhere secure," offered Pooh.

"Sssomewhere sssecret, sssonny!" added Gopher.

Pooh and the gang carried the chest to Piglet's house. Once the place was protected, they set the chest down and tried to pry it open with a pole.

"I can't wait!" said Pooh. "What do you suppose is inside?"

"Probably a whole bunch of fun stuff," replied Tigger.

"But then again," said Pooh, hopefully, "it could be honey."

"Honey, Pooh?" said Piglet, bending the pole as far back as it would go.

"Well," said Pooh, grabbing the pole to help Piglet. "I'd fill a treasure chest with honey!"

Suddenly, the pole snapped back, flipping Pooh and Piglet up in the air.

Pooh and Piglet fell back to the ground. As they dusted themselves off from their fall, Tigger and Gopher thought of another way to get the chest open.

The two disappeared into the wood and returned lugging a giant log. Then, on the count of three, they charged at the chest. Unfortunately, they completely missed it, and crashed into Piglet's front door, instead.

"Oh, d-dear!" cried Piglet.

Next, they tried to break the chest open by dropping it from the ceiling. But when they let the chest go, it crashed straight through the floor.

"Where'd it go?" asked Piglet.

"To the basement," answered Tigger.

"But I don't have a basement," said Piglet.

Tigger grinned sheepishly. "You do now!" he said.

"I've got it!" said Gopher. "Tomorrow, when it's light enough for us to see what we're doing, we'll blast the thing open with dynamite!"

Rabbit had watched all that went on through Piglet's window, and he couldn't have been more pleased with himself.

"I never dreamed the trick would turn out so well!" Rabbit said to himself when he got home. "When they find that chest is full of rocks, they'll think twice about tearing up gardens!"

Rabbit pulled back the covers on his bed. "Ah, Rabbit, you are a genius! An absolute genius!" he yawned, lying down for a nap.

Still wearing a smile on his face, Rabbit drifted off to sleep, and soon found himself in the middle of a strange dream.

Rabbit dreamed he was surrounded by giant talking rocks shaped a lot like Pooh, Piglet, Tigger and Gopher. The rocks seemed to glare at him.

"It wasn't very n-nice giving us a fake t-treasure," said Piglet Rock.

"You built up all our hopes," accused Pooh Rock.

"You got us all exciterated!" exploded Tigger Rock.

"And what'd we get? A bunch of rocks!" shouted Gopher Rock.

Frightened, Rabbit went down on his knees, begging for mercy. "I-I'm sorry! It was a joke!" explained Rabbit. "It was just a joke!"

"It was a joke, just a joke!" Rabbit muttered in his sleep. Then his eyes popped open, and he sat bolt upright in bed.

"Oh!" said Rabbit, looking around the room. "It was just a bad dream!"

Rabbit got out of bed and began to pace the floor with his head in his hands.

"Oh, what have I done?" he groaned. "When they find out what's in that chest, they'll hate me forever! Unless," said Rabbit, suddenly hopeful, "unless I get it back before they open it! But how?"

Rabbit thought for a long time before he came up with an idea.

Later that day, Piglet panicked when he looked out the window and saw the ghost of Long John Cottontail. Actually, it was Rabbit dressed up to look like his great-great-great uncle.

"Harrrr!" growled Rabbit, "I've come for what's mine!"

"Er, you better go talk to him, Captain Piglet!" said Tigger, frightened.

"P-perhaps we sh-should just give him his treasure," suggested Piglet.

Gopher didn't want to give up the chest, and neither did Pooh. Instead, they lowered the drawbridge on Rabbit's head, flattening him.

"Goodness!" said Pooh, peering out. "He seems to have disappeared!"

"Well, let's open the chest before that ghostie comes back!" said Tigger.

Defeated, Rabbit dragged himself to the window and looked in.

"Don't forget," said Piglet. "We must share the treasure with Rabbit."

"Share…with me?" thought Rabbit, listening.

"If Rabbit hadn't shown us where to d-dig, we never would've found the t-treasure," said Captain Piglet. "Part of it is his."

Rabbit shook his head sadly, turning away. "When they see those rocks, they'll never speak to me again!" thought Rabbit. "The only thing left for me to do is move away."

The next morning, Rabbit hurriedly packed up his belongings. He was tossing everything onto a wagon when Pooh and Tigger walked up.

"Rabbit! Rabbit!" called Pooh and Tigger. Neither of them seemed to notice the wagon overflowing with Rabbit's belongings. "We're going to open the treasure," said Pooh, grabbing Rabbit by the arm. "Come on!"

"No! No! I don't want any part of it!" protested Rabbit.

"He doesn't want any part of it! What an unselfish guy!" said Tigger.

Pooh and Tigger dragged Rabbit near Pooh's house. Rabbit's eyes widened when he saw the chest surrounded by bundles of dynamite. Gopher was wiring the dynamite to set off the explosion, and Piglet watched.

"No, no, please, no!" cried Rabbit.

"Aww, don't worry," said Gopher. "One push of this dingie and the whole thing goes kabingie! Ten, nine, eight, blassst off!"

Gopher pushed the plunger.

"NOOOO!" shouted Rabbit.

Finally, the chest was open. Rabbit tried to cover it with his body. "No! Don't look!" said Rabbit, thinking quickly. "Uncle Long John's such a kidder! Probably put the treasure in some other chest!"

Looking at Rabbit strangely, Tigger started to pry Rabbit's arms off the chest. Rabbit grabbed for the chest again, with a desperate look on his face.

"No! He…he…he forgot to put a treasure in it!" said Rabbit, talking very fast. "Uncle Long John—so absent-minded—buried an empty chest!"

"Oh, all right!" cried Rabbit. "I confess! It was me! I put the rocks in there!" Rabbit waited for his friends to yell at him, but they said nothing. "There never was a treasure!" said Rabbit. "I'm sorry. I'm sorry!"

Piglet and the others were confused. Ignoring Rabbit, they inched up to the chest and looked inside.

"This will keep my chair from wobbling!" said Pooh, grabbing a rock.

"Jussst what I need to prop up my winchbolts!" declared Gopher.

"Fantastical!" breathed Tigger. "What a great nutcracker!"

"It's every treasure we ever dreamed of!" said Piglet.

Rabbit pointed to the rocks in disbelief. "But, they're only…"

"And this is your share, Bunny Boy," said Tigger, handing one of the rocks to Rabbit.

"But, uh…but…"

"It's all right," said Piglet. "You take it—though it *is* a rare and valuable doorstop…"

"Probably belonged to your Uncle Long John!" guessed Tigger.

Rabbit was touched. "Why, I hardly know what to say," began Rabbit.

"But we do," said Piglet. "Thank you for helping us find this treasure."

"And thank you for this rare and valuable, uh, doorstop," said Rabbit.

While the group stood around the treasure chest, admiring their rocks, a ghost appeared from out of nowhere.

"A-har! Ya found me buried rocks, didya?" said Long John.

"Ghoooooooost!" yelled Rabbit, Tigger, Piglet and Pooh and Gopher. And they all ran for their lives.